THE QUEEN'S PRESENT

Steve Antony

Hodder
Children's
Books

It was **Christmas Eve** and the Queen
still hadn't found the perfect present
for the little prince and princess.

Luckily, someone special was
just around the corner to help...

Father Christmas flew down the
street and in a whistle they were off...

around the world in search
of the perfect present!

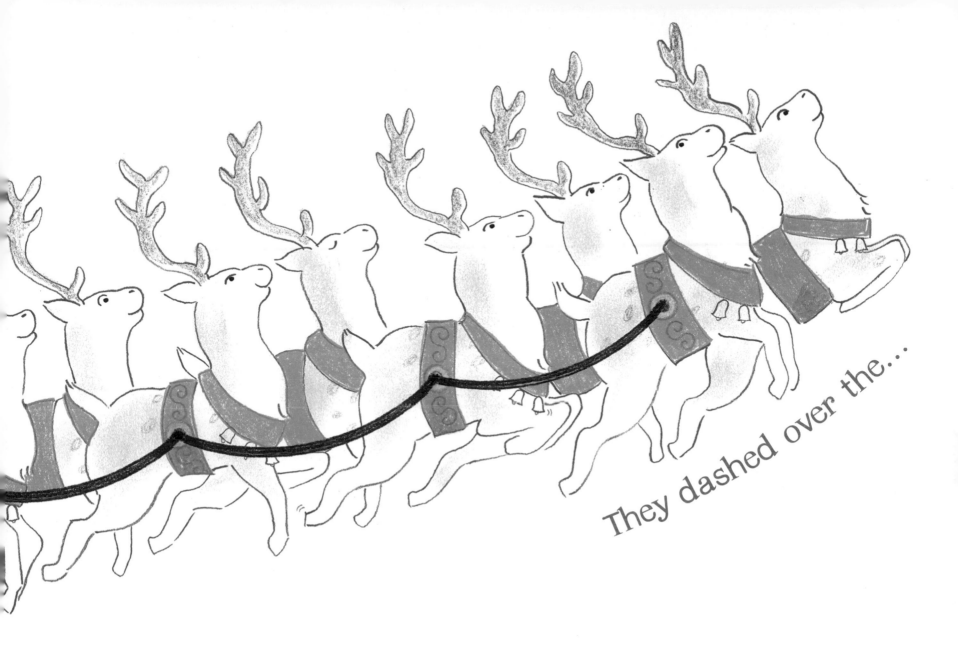

They dashed over the...

Eiffel Tower in Paris.

They pranced around the...

Leaning Tower of Pisa.

They soared up to the...

Great Pyramids of Egypt.

They glided along the...

Great Wall of China.

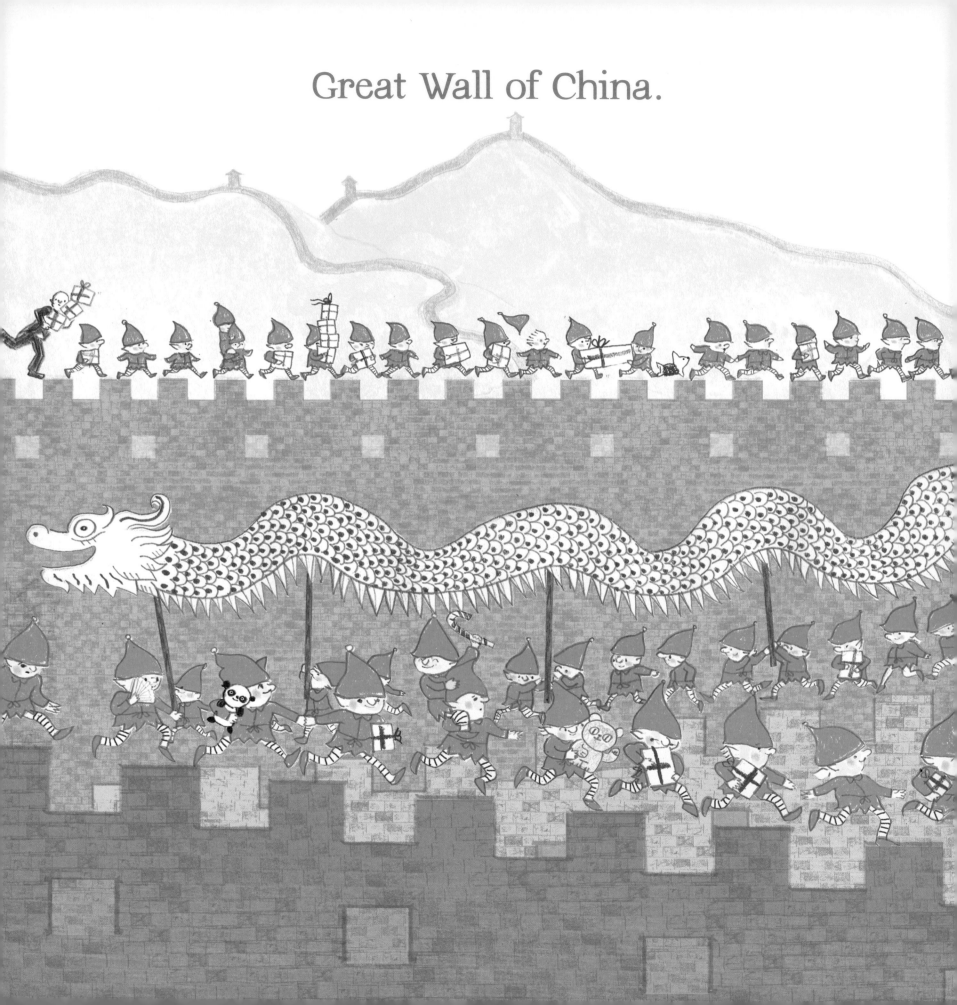

They darted past the...

Himeji Castle in Japan.

They swooped to the...

Sydney Opera House
in Australia.

They flew over the…

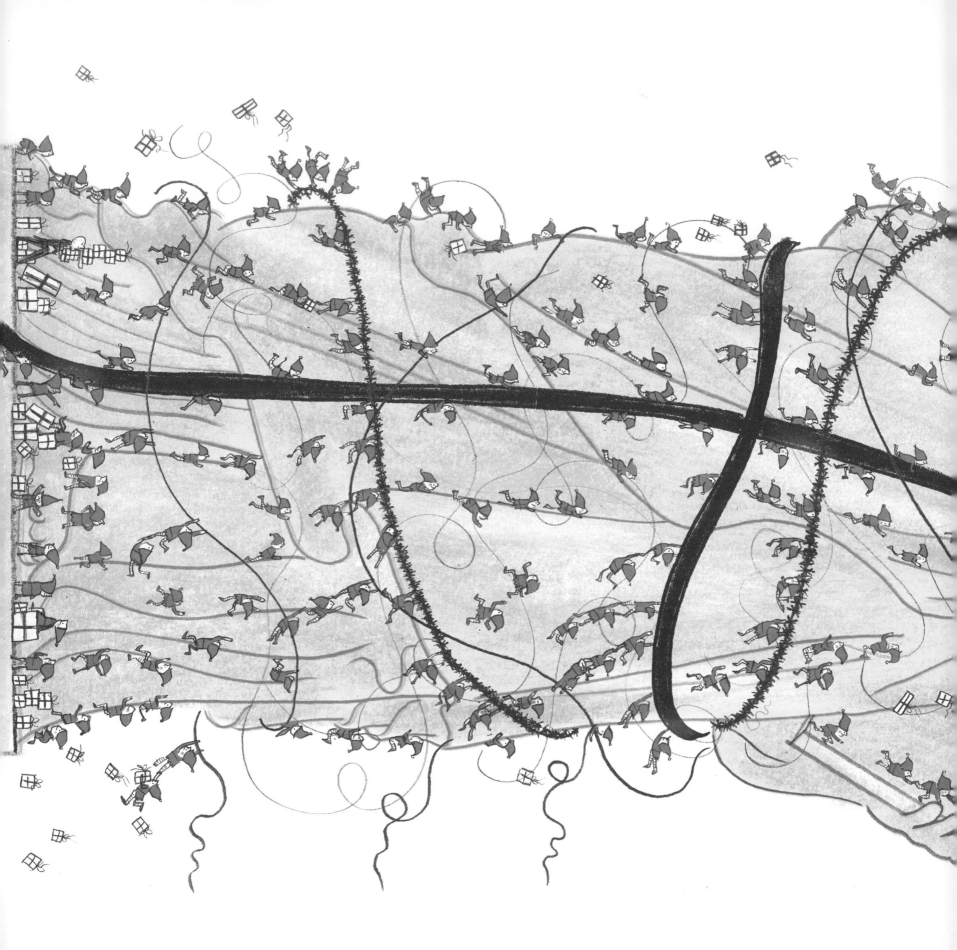

Statue of Liberty and all the way to...

The North Pole,

but they still couldn't find the perfect present.

It was nearly Christmas Day so Father Christmas took the Queen home to...

Sandringham House in England,

where the little prince and princess
received the best present of all...

a Christmas cuddle
from Grandma.